My First

Christmas Carols

Mary E. Erickson
Illustrated by Bari Weissman

Chariot Books
A Division of Cook
Communications Ministries

In Bethlehem

Mary E. Erickson

Lewis H. Redner

In grass - y fields near Beth - le - hem, the

shep- herds kept their sheep. An an - gel bright and

shin - ing woke the shep- herds from their

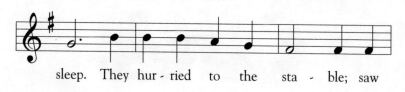

sleep. They hur - ried to the sta - ble; saw

ORIGINAL CAROL: "O Little Town of Bethlehem"

4

Je - sus in the hay. Be - side the man - ger,

shep - herds knelt to wor - ship and to pray.

Jesus Christ Is Born

Mary E. Erickson

Franz Grüber

Tranquillo

Si - lent night! Ho - ly night!

An - gels sing; stars are bright. Moth-er Ma - ry is

filled with great joy. God's own Son is her

first ba - by boy. Je - sus Christ is

born. Je - sus Christ is born.

ORIGINAL CAROL: "Silent Night"

Mary's Lullaby

Mary E. Erickson

Cheri Potter

Softly

1. Close your eyes, my ba-by. Rest your lit-tle head,
2. Close your eyes, my ba-by. You are God's own Son.

with the lamb and don-key near your man-ger bed.
He sent You to teach us to love eve-ry-one.

Sleep my ba-by Je-sus, on the soft warm hay,
Sleep my ba-by Je-sus, while your star shines bright.

while the shep-herds tell their friends, "Christ was born to-day."
Chil-dren will re-mem-ber You on this spe-cial night.

Refrain

Sleep my ba-by Je-sus, while your star shines bright.

Chil-dren will re-mem-ber You on this spe-cial night.

My Gift to Jesus

Mary E. Erickson

Traditional Melody

On Christ - mas Eve, this

car - ol I sing: "A - way in a

man - ger, no crib for the King." I

can't give Him my room or my

bed. But I can give Je - sus my

ORIGINAL CAROL: "The First Noel"

heart in - stead. My heart, my heart! My heart, my heart! I will give Je - sus all my heart.

Good News from On High

Mary E. Erickson

Richard S. Willis

While shep-herds guarded the sheep one night, they

saw a light in the sky. "Don't be a-fraid," an

an-gel said. "I bring good news from on high. In

ORIGINAL CAROL: "It Came Upon the Midnight Clear"

12

Beth-le-hem   is   born   to-night   a
ba-by that shall   be king.   You'll find Him in   a
man-ger bed. Now hear the   an - gels   sing."

13

The Angels' Song

Mary E. Erickson   Felix Mendelssohn

Lis-ten to the an-gels sing   songs a-bout the

new-born King. Prais-ing God in heaven a-bove,

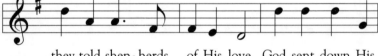

they told shep-herds   of His love. God sent down His

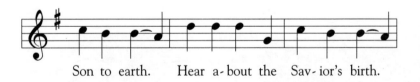

Son to earth.   Hear a-bout the Sav-ior's birth.

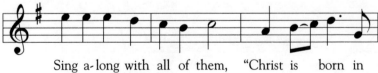

Sing a-long with all of them, "Christ is   born in

ORIGINAL CAROL: "Hark! The Herald Angels Sing"

14

Beth-le-hem." Lis - ten to the an-gels sing.

Wor - ship Christ, the new-born King.

Telling the Story

Mary E. Erickson   Henry Smart

1. Shep-herds left the man-ger ba - by. They went out o'er
2. I   can be just like the shep-herds. I can tell a -

all   the earth. Full of   joy, they told the sto- ry
bout God's love. How God sent His Son to save us;

of   God's   love   and   Je - sus' birth.
sent   Him   down   from   heav'n a - bove.

Refrain

Come   and wor-ship! Come   and   wor-ship!

Wor - ship   Je - sus,   God's own Son.

ORIGINAL CAROL: "Angels from the Realms of Glory"

16

Star So Bright

Mary E. Erickson

John H. Hopkins

We three kings one night saw a star.

Cam - els car - ried us from a - far.

Through hot de - serts, o - ver moun - tains,

we fol- lowed that bright star. Oh, —

ORIGINAL CAROL: "We Three Kings of Orient Are"

18

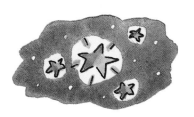

star so bril-liant, star so bright,

guid-ed three kings through the night.

We gave pre-cious gifts to Je-sus.

Then we wor-shiped Christ, God's Light.

Christ Is King

Mary E. Erickson

G. F. Handel

When church bells chime at Christ-mas - time, then

we will go to church, to sing a-bout the

ba - by, who slept in a man - ger. We'll

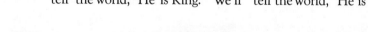

tell the world, "He is King." We'll tell the world, "He is

King." We'll tell the world that "Christ is King."

ORIGINAL CAROL: "Joy to the World"

O Come, Little Children

Mary E. Erickson

Wade's Cantus Diversi

O come, lit - tle chil - dren.

Come and wor-ship Je - sus. O come, lit - tle

chil - dren, to Beth - le - hem. Come, wor-ship

Je - sus. Kneel be-side the man - ger.

ORIGINAL CAROL: "O Come, All Ye Faithful"

O   come and sing for   Je - sus. O

come and pray to   Je - sus,   O come and wor-ship

Je - sus,   Christ   the   Lord.

I Love You

Carrie B. Williams

Carrie B. Williams

1. Lit - tle ba - by in the man - ger, "I love you!"
2. We may hear the Sav - ior say - ing, "I love you."

Ly - ing there, to earth a stran - ger, "I love you."
In our sleep - ing, in our play - ing, "I love you."

Wise men saw the star, and an - swered, "I love you."
In the dark or in the day - time, "I love you."

Shep - herds heard the an - gels sing - ing, "I love you."
'Tis the gen - tle shep - herd say - ing, "I love you."

Trim the Tree

Mary E. Erickson   Old Welsh Air

Trim the tree with lights and tin-sel. Fa la la la la, la

la la la. On the top, let's put an angel. Fa la la la la, la

la la la. "Mer-ry Christ-mas," we will all say.

ORIGINAL CAROL: "Deck the Halls"

26

Fa la la, la la la, la la la. Then we'll cel - e -

brate Christ's birth - day. Fa la la la la, la la la la.

God Loves Children Everywhere

Mary E. Erickson

An English Carol

God   loves the chil-dren ev' - ry-where, and

He wants us   to   know   that He sent Je - sus

ORIGINAL CAROL: "God Rest Ye Merry, Gentlemen"

to our world be - cause He loves us so. Let's

tell the Christ- mas sto - ry wher - ev - er we may

go.   Oh   sto - ry   of

Je - sus and love,   Je - sus and love.   Oh

sto - ry of Je - sus and love.

Christmas Bells

Mary E. Erickson   J. Baptiste Calkin

I   hear the bells on Christ-mas Day and

sing the car-ols that they play. I   like   the mu-sic

of the bells and stor-ies that the   Bi - ble tells.

ORIGINAL CAROL: "I Heard the Bells on Christmas Day"